LaShon Ormond

The Hummingbird who wanted To Sing

To the girls who have
brought songs to my heart:
Jasmyne, Kirsten Marie, Madison, McKenzie,
Laniya, Lateya, Emily, and Desire.

The Hummingbird who wanted To Sing

Harmony was a
hummingbird
The tiniest thing
With a beak and with feathers
And these amazing wings.

Harmony could fly
Nearly thirty miles
per hour...

And dive going sixty
From the tallest of towers.

With this incredible speed
And these fantastic wings...

Harmony was still sad
Because she
could not sing.

Harmony could chirp

And when flying she hummed

But Harmony believed in her heart

There was a song to be sung.

Harmony had feathers

And iridescent colors so bright

But all she really wanted was a song

She could sing in the night.

One day Harmony asked her mother

why hummingbirds did not sing.

Harmony's mom looked at

her daughter and said,

"Why Harmony, what on earth

do you mean?"

"Do you not hear

The song that you play...

When you're flapping your wings

On a warm spring day?"

And do you not know
The joy that you bring

When between sips of
nectar you drink,
you are continuously
chirping?"

"

My Dear, that is your song
And it is a beautiful one

That you give to the flowers
And the non-flying ones.

"It's like the gift you give

By rubbing your head on each blossom

Oh Harmony, you have a song

And the world thinks it's awesome!

And with that

Harmony smiled

And she started to think

About her gifts to the world

And her desire for singing started to shrink.

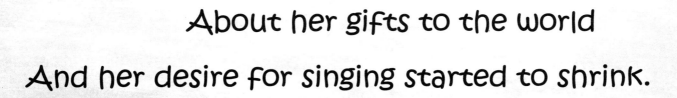

As she listened to her song

At the flap of her wings,

Harmony realized she had been

gifted with so many things.

She could fly forward and backwards

Something her friend Robin could not do...

And she could see far, far away

And hide her colors when she needed to.

Harmony realized that she had a beautiful song

Hidden in her wings, and that is the song

That Harmony the
Hummingbird sings!

Made in the USA
Columbia, SC
27 March 2024

33644398R10015